MYTHOLOGICAL CREATURES

A CLASSICAL BESTIARY

TALES OF STRANGE BEINGS,
FABULOUS CREATURES,
FEARSOME BEASTS,
& HIDEOUS MONSTERS
FROM ANCIENT GREEK MYTHOLOGY

LYNN CURLEE

ATHENEUM BOOKS FOR YOUNG READERS
NEW YORK LONDON TORONTO SYDNEY

PROLOGUE

In ancient Greece people told wonderful stories of a magical world. It was a place ruled by powerful gods and goddesses, where brave heroes performed astonishing deeds for great kings. To the early Greeks this world was real. The stories reflected their history and their religion, for they revered the legendary kings and heroes as ancestors, and they worshipped the gods and goddesses. These wonderful stories are called myths.

The Greek myths were passed from generation to generation. Parents taught them to their children, bards recited them in village squares, and in the halls of kings, minstrels plucked lyres as they sang stirring sagas of gods and heroes. Finally the myths were written down. Poets composed splendid epics about wars, ocean voyages, and feats of valor. Playwrights wrote tragic dramas of love, betrayal, murder, and revenge, while other authors told charming fables. Sculptors and painters adorned marble temples with beautiful images inspired by the ancient legends. Some of the poems, plays, paintings, and sculpture survived through the centuries. This is how we still know the myths today.

Besides gods, kings, and heroes, the Greek myths are also full of strange beings and fabulous creatures. Some of these are like characters from a beautiful dream; others are simply amusing or bizarre. But there are also fearsome beasts and hideous monsters so terrible and grotesque that they seem drawn from our deepest, darkest nightmares. During the Middle Ages, more than a millennium after the ancient Greeks, in an era when the myths were almost forgotten, people collected stories about real or imaginary animals in books called bestiaries. Here is a collection of tales about amazing imaginary creatures from ancient Greek mythology—a classical bestiary.

Pan, the God of Nature

The greatest of the gods and goddesses lived in splendor at the summit of Mount Olympus, but for shepherds and hunters there was a god who lived closer to home. Greece is a country of rugged mountains that rise up out of the sea. There are rocky hills and green valleys, meadows and woodlands, olive groves, wild grapevines, and sparkling streams. This was the domain of Pan, the god of nature. The Olympian gods were handsome, but Pan looked very odd, with the hairy haunches and cloven hooves of a goat. He even had pointed ears, horns, and a tail. Perhaps because of this he preferred wild, remote places and was seldom seen by men.

Pan's countryside was also home to nymphs, spirits of trees, rocks, and streams that took the form of young women. Pan was always falling in love with this nymph or that, but they merely laughed at him. One day Pan came upon the most beautiful nymph he had ever seen. Her name was Syrinx. She ran away, and Pan chased her to the edge of a stream. She quickly changed herself into a slim reed, like hundreds of others on the riverbank. Pan was crestfallen, for he had fallen deeply in love. But when he heard the wind rustling the reeds, the sound was so enchanting that he gathered some reeds and blew through them to re-create it.

After that Pan always carried his reed pipes, playing gay tunes when he felt happy, but making somber music when he was sad. For even though he was a god, Pan was very lonely. Sometimes he was overcome with despair and simply sat in a dark cave, howling like a wounded animal. His echoing cries were so bloodcurdling that anyone who heard them was gripped by a terrible fear known as *panic*.

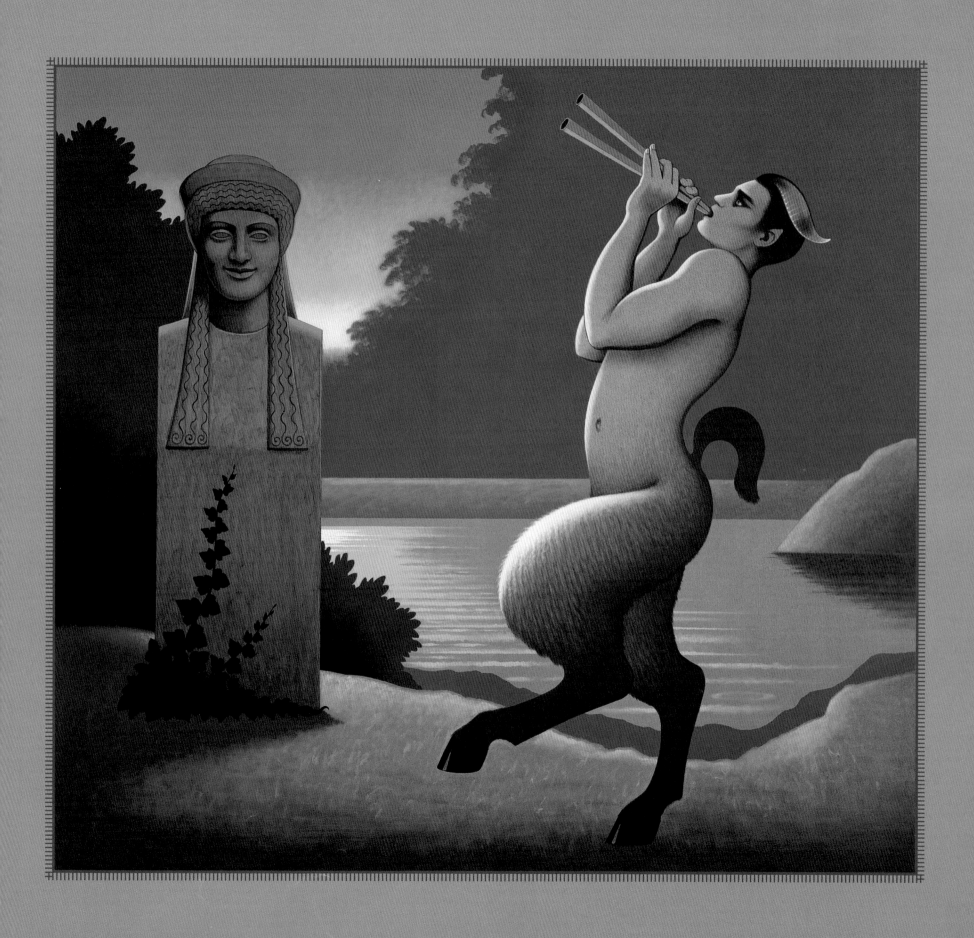

Centaurs

Tribes of Centaurs lived in the countryside as well. They were not spirits, but creatures of flesh and blood, half man and half horse, half tame and half wild. Their manners were coarse, and they laughed at the laws and rules of men. When the Centaurs drank too much of their strong wine, they became rude and belligerent, stampeding about in herds, destroying crops and uprooting trees. It was even said that they fed on raw meat.

On one occasion the Centaurs were invited to a wedding feast given by the Lapiths, their human neighbors. At first they were polite and cordial, but as the wine flowed, the Centaurs became more and more obnoxious, staggering around insulting the other guests and chasing bridesmaids. One even tried to drag away the bride herself. Enraged, the Lapith men attacked the Centaurs to drive them off. Since they were so intoxicated, the battle was a rout in which many Centaurs were wounded or killed. The Lapiths later drove the rest of the Centaurs from Greece. The famous battle between the Lapiths and the Centaurs was a favorite subject for Greek artists.

But there was one Centaur who was completely different from his brethren. Chiron was the Centaur king. He lived far away from the others on Mount Pelion. Chiron was gentle and kind and very old and wise. He was a master healer, and he was also famed as the most distinguished tutor in all of Greece. Many boys who grew up to be great heroes spent their youth in his charge, where they learned the arts of mathematics, gymnastics, archery, and music. Although he was a healer, when Chiron was accidentally pricked by a poisoned arrow, he was unable to heal himself. After he died, the gods honored his memory by placing him in the heavens as a constellation of stars, twinkling in the night sky.

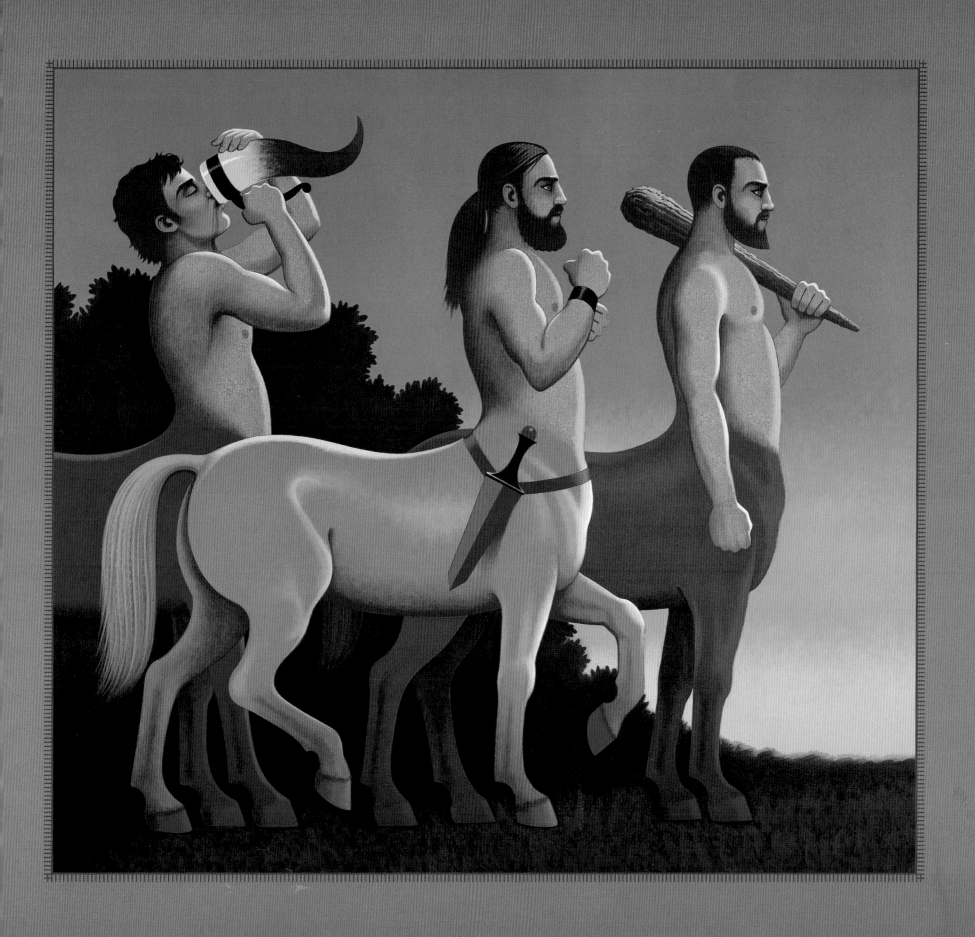

Triton, the Herald of Poseidon

The gods and goddesses were all related to one another, and like most families, they sometimes bickered among themselves. To avoid arguments the three eldest brothers carved the universe into three kingdoms. Zeus was lord of the heavens and the most powerful of all the gods. His brother Hades ruled the underworld—the land of the dead—a dark and dismal place beneath the earth, far from the glory of Olympus. The third brother was Poseidon, master of the seas. Poseidon divided his time between Mount Olympus and a grand palace of coral studded with pearls and golden nuggets in the watery depths of his kingdom. From his palace Poseidon could actually shake the earth itself, causing even the strongest men to tremble with fear.

Poseidon traveled with an entourage of sea creatures led by his son Triton, who had the form of a powerfully built young man with scaly tail fins instead of legs. Accompanied by sea nymphs, dolphins, and flying fish, Triton served as his father's herald. He rode out in front of Poseidon's water chariot on the back of a hippocampus, a kind of sea horse with flippers and a powerful fish tail. Triton announced the arrivals and departures of the great sea god with sharp, piercing blasts on his spiral shell trumpet.

Triton also had the honor of serving as the bearer of Poseidon's trident, a scepter with three prongs. At the god's command Triton could wave it to calm the seas until they were as smooth as glass. But Poseidon was moody and violent, prone to terrible outbursts of temper. When he was angry, he would order Triton to call up raging hurricanes, with howling winds and great, crashing waves.

Gryphons

Persia was an exotic land far from Greece, across the Aegean Sea and beyond the eastern mountains. It was a rugged place, with lofty, snow-covered peaks that were home to astonishing creatures called Gryphons. These fabulous beasts had the bodies of lions and the heads of huge birds, with elaborate crests and golden beaks. Their dazzling, iridescent wings beat the air with an unearthly whirring noise when they took flight. Otherwise they were totally silent, never uttering a sound.

Gryphons built enormous nests of finely spun golden wire at the very summits of the most remote mountains. Their large eggs had shells veined with gold and studded with jewels, and during their entire lives, each pair of Gryphons produced only one egg. As a result these wonderful creatures were incredibly rare. In fact, Gryphons were so seldom seen that many claimed that they did not even exist.

Persian kings kept Gryphons to guard secret treasure chambers, where it was rumored they kept a collection of intact Gryphon eggs, the rarest, most precious treasure of all. When one of these guardian Gryphons died, its golden talons were removed and hollowed out to be fashioned into elaborate drinking cups, which were reserved only for Persian royalty.

The great god Zeus kept a pair of Gryphons on Mount Olympus. He fed them with his own hands, and he tamed them and trained them to sit at the base of his throne like a pair of enormous pet dogs. On ceremonial occasions his wife, Hera, used them to draw her golden sky chariot, which made her the envy of all the other goddesses.

Argus, the Watchman with One Hundred Eyes

Although they were married, Zeus and Hera were not in love. She was a stately goddess who was very vain and proud, but she was a nagging wife. For his part, Zeus was always slipping away to earth for love affairs with mortal women or nymphs, which understandably infuriated Hera.

Once, Zeus fell in love with a princess named Io. When Hera became suspicious, Zeus changed Io into a cow to avoid his wife's wrath. Since Io was very beautiful, with lovely pale skin, she became a beautiful white cow, but a cow nonetheless. Hera was not deceived. She asked for the beautiful cow as a gift, and of course Zeus could not refuse. Then Hera sent a watchman to keep Io prisoner. His name was Argus, and he was a particularly good watchman, for in addition to his two eyes in their normal sockets, he had ninety-eight other eyes scattered over his body. Since his one hundred eyes slept at different times, it was impossible for Io to escape.

Zeus wanted to help, so he sent the god Hermes to rescue her. Hermes was the patron of merchants and travelers, and he served as Zeus's personal messenger. He was the most cunning and sly of all the gods, and with wings on his cap and his feet, he was the swiftest as well. Hermes made friends with Argus. As they sat together watching Io, Hermes told stories. He made sure to speak slowly and softly, droning on and on, until Argus became bored and sleepy, his eyes winking shut one by one. As soon as he heard snores, Hermes took his sword and sliced off Argus's head. Io was free, but Zeus let her remain a cow to protect her from Hera's anger. And so that Zeus could never forget his infidelity, Hera took Argus's eyes and scattered them throughout the tail feathers of her favorite bird, the peacock.

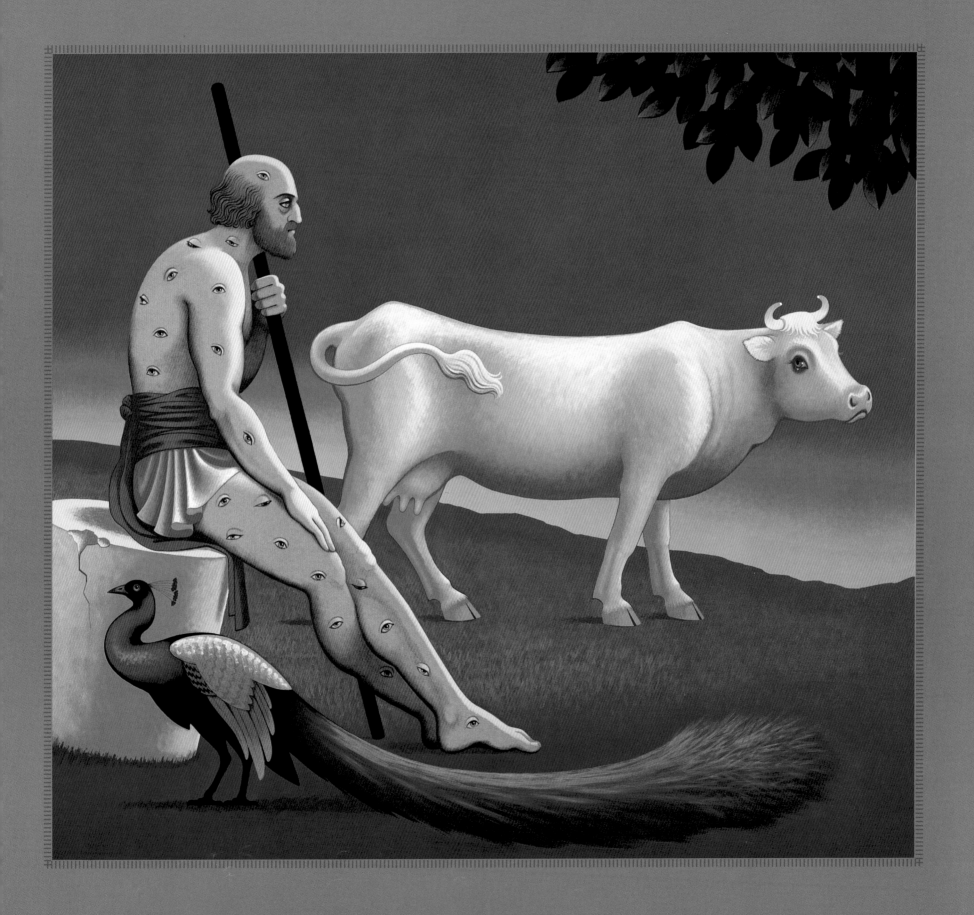

The Sphinx

Thebes was a prosperous Greek city, famous for its lofty stone walls and seven gates. But when its people neglected to worship the great goddess Hera, she sent a terrible demon to punish them. The Sphinx had the face and flowing hair of a beautiful woman, but she had the muscular body and cruel claws of a powerful lioness and the wings of a huge bird. The monstrous creature nested on top of the city ramparts and flew down to block the road whenever anyone tried to approach one of the gates. She would then ask a riddle. If the wrong answer was given, the Sphinx tore apart the unfortunate traveler and devoured him. Since no one knew how to solve the puzzle, many people were killed and eaten. After a time the people of Thebes began to starve, for no food could be brought into the city.

One day a young traveler named Oedipus approached Thebes. From her high perch the Sphinx saw him coming and swooped down on her great wings to block his path. "What creature goes on four legs at dawn, two legs during the day, and three legs at dusk?" she demanded.

Oedipus thought for a moment, then responded: "The answer is human beings. As babies we crawl on all fours, for most of our lives we walk upright on two legs, and when we are old, we use a staff as a third leg to support ourselves." The Sphinx's face darkened with rage and she let out a savage roar, for Oedipus had given the correct answer. Then she flew to the top of the lofty citadel and flung herself onto the rocks below. She was killed instantly and Hera's curse was lifted. Oedipus was a good and noble young man, and in thanks the people of Thebes proclaimed him their king.

Polyphemus, the Cyclops

The Greek army sailed across the Aegean Sea on a thousand ships to make war against the city of Troy in Asia Minor. After ten years of bloodshed the war was over and Troy was in ashes. But in their victory the Greeks forgot to properly honor the gods, so Poseidon sent a hurricane to destroy their fleet. Tossed in every direction, only a few ships survived. One of them belonged to Odysseus, a Greek general, now lost with his men upon the vast ocean.

One day they landed on a rocky island and decided to spend the night in a warm cave, little knowing that the island belonged to the Cyclopes, a tribe of brutish giants. The cave was home to Polyphemus, a shepherd. Like all Cyclopes, he was tall as an oak and his limbs were as thick as tree trunks. He had but one staring eye in the middle of his face, and his favorite food was human flesh. When he returned and discovered the Greeks in his cave, Polyphemus took two of the men and devoured them, bones and all. The next morning when he left with his goats, the Cyclops rolled a huge boulder over the cave entrance to imprison the rest of the Greeks. Then when he returned that evening, he ate two more men.

Odysseus dared not kill the Cyclops while he slept, for only the giant could move the boulder. So the next night he offered Polyphemus some strong wine. After the Cyclops had drunk himself into a stupor, Odysseus took a sharpened stake and thrust it deep into the giant's horrible eye. Polyphemus shrieked in agony and staggered around, blindly groping for the men, but they hid among the goats. The next day when the blinded Cyclops let out his flock, Odysseus and his men escaped by clinging upside down to the wool on the goats' bellies, where the giant could not feel them.

The Ram with a Golden Fleece

Phrixus and Helle were the young son and daughter of King Athamas. Their mother was a cloud nymph named Nephele, and although she dearly loved her children, she was of the sky and could not live on earth with them. Eventually the king took a new wife. Queen Ino was consumed by jealousy for the prince and princess and plotted to have them killed. From her home in the sky Nephele could see into the queen's wicked heart, and she prayed that her children be saved.

Zeus heard her prayers and sent his messenger Hermes to rescue the children. The god brought with him a wondrous magical ram. This amazing creature had magnificent spiraling horns of solid gold and a thick, shining fleece of glittering golden wool. Hermes lifted Phrixus and Helle onto its back, and immediately the ram leaped into the air and soared away, for Zeus had granted it the ability to fly. At first it was an exciting adventure for the children. With the wind in their faces, they held tightly to the gleaming wool as they flew over the countryside. But as the ram headed out over the ocean, Helle became very tired and frightened. She lost her grip and plunged into the sea far below, but Phrixus wrapped his arms more tightly around the ram's neck and held on.

They finally landed far from Greece in the kingdom of Colchis, where Phrixus sacrificed the golden ram as an offering to Zeus. The young prince then presented the hide to the king of Colchis, who hung it in a grove of trees sacred to Ares, the god of war. This grove was the lair of a huge, coiling serpent that never slept, so the Golden Fleece was very well guarded. There it remained for many years—the greatest treasure of the kingdom.

The Harpies

In Greece rumors had spread about the priceless Golden Fleece. An ambitious youth named Jason resolved to go and bring it back, and he recruited a band of brave young men to join him. Colchis was hundreds of miles away, so Jason constructed the largest ship yet built. He named it the *Argo*, his crew called themselves Argonauts, and they set out upon an epic quest for the Golden Fleece.

One night the *Argo* anchored near the palace of King Phineus of Thrace. The old king possessed the gift of prophecy, but since Zeus preferred that men not know the future, the great god had sent a plague of terrible creatures called Harpies to torture Phineus. The Harpies were also known as the *Hounds of Zeus*, but they were not dogs. They had the bodies and wings of vultures and the heads of ugly old crones. Phineus was fabulously wealthy, but he led a miserable existence, for whenever he tried to eat from his golden plates, the Harpies swooped down, screeching in his ears, flapping their wings in his face, and snatching the food from his hands. They left a vile stench so disgusting that it made Phineus ill. By the time the Argonauts finally came upon him, he was reduced nearly to skin and bones.

Among the Argonauts were the twins Calais and Zetes. They were sons of the North Wind and very swift. When the Harpies appeared at the next meal, the twins were waiting with drawn swords. They gave a great shout, and the Harpies flew away squawking in alarm, with the twins in hot pursuit. They would have killed the repulsive creatures, but suddenly the goddess Iris appeared in a rainbow with a message from Zeus. If the Harpies were spared, he promised they would never return. In gratitude Phineus helped the Argonauts by telling them what would happen next on their journey, and after many more adventures they finally reached Colchis.

The Harpies

In Greece rumors had spread about the priceless Golden Fleece. An ambitious youth named Jason resolved to go and bring it back, and he recruited a band of brave young men to join him. Colchis was hundreds of miles away, so Jason constructed the largest ship yet built. He named it the *Argo*, his crew called themselves Argonauts, and they set out upon an epic quest for the Golden Fleece.

One night the *Argo* anchored near the palace of King Phineus of Thrace. The old king possessed the gift of prophecy, but since Zeus preferred that men not know the future, the great god had sent a plague of terrible creatures called Harpies to torture Phineus. The Harpies were also known as the *Hounds of Zeus*, but they were not dogs. They had the bodies and wings of vultures and the heads of ugly old crones. Phineus was fabulously wealthy, but he led a miserable existence, for whenever he tried to eat from his golden plates, the Harpies swooped down, screeching in his ears, flapping their wings in his face, and snatching the food from his hands. They left a vile stench so disgusting that it made Phineus ill. By the time the Argonauts finally came upon him, he was reduced nearly to skin and bones.

Among the Argonauts were the twins Calais and Zetes. They were sons of the North Wind and very swift. When the Harpies appeared at the next meal, the twins were waiting with drawn swords. They gave a great shout, and the Harpies flew away squawking in alarm, with the twins in hot pursuit. They would have killed the repulsive creatures, but suddenly the goddess Iris appeared in a rainbow with a message from Zeus. If the Harpies were spared, he promised they would never return. In gratitude Phineus helped the Argonauts by telling them what would happen next on their journey, and after many more adventures they finally reached Colchis.

The Harpies

In Greece rumors had spread about the priceless Golden Fleece. An ambitious youth named Jason resolved to go and bring it back, and he recruited a band of brave young men to join him. Colchis was hundreds of miles away, so Jason constructed the largest ship yet built. He named it the *Argo*, his crew called themselves Argonauts, and they set out upon an epic quest for the Golden Fleece.

One night the *Argo* anchored near the palace of King Phineus of Thrace. The old king possessed the gift of prophecy, but since Zeus preferred that men not know the future, the great god had sent a plague of terrible creatures called Harpies to torture Phineus. The Harpies were also known as the *Hounds of Zeus*, but they were not dogs. They had the bodies and wings of vultures and the heads of ugly old crones. Phineus was fabulously wealthy, but he led a miserable existence, for whenever he tried to eat from his golden plates, the Harpies swooped down, screeching in his ears, flapping their wings in his face, and snatching the food from his hands. They left a vile stench so disgusting that it made Phineus ill. By the time the Argonauts finally came upon him, he was reduced nearly to skin and bones.

Among the Argonauts were the twins Calais and Zetes. They were sons of the North Wind and very swift. When the Harpies appeared at the next meal, the twins were waiting with drawn swords. They gave a great shout, and the Harpies flew away squawking in alarm, with the twins in hot pursuit. They would have killed the repulsive creatures, but suddenly the goddess Iris appeared in a rainbow with a message from Zeus. If the Harpies were spared, he promised they would never return. In gratitude Phineus helped the Argonauts by telling them what would happen next on their journey, and after many more adventures they finally reached Colchis.

Talus, the Bronze Giant

Princess Medea of Colchis was a sorceress. When she first saw Jason, she fell deeply in love and decided to use her dark magic to help him in his quest for the Golden Fleece. In Ares' sacred grove she cast a spell, causing the serpent to fall into a deep sleep. Jason grabbed the fleece, and they fled in the *Argo*. When Medea's treachery was discovered, her brother Prince Apsyrtus pursued the thieves, but together Medea and Jason killed him and escaped.

On the voyage to Greece they sailed near Crete, an island kingdom guarded by a fierce warrior giant named Talus. He endlessly patrolled the cliffs, and when a strange ship approached, he pelted it with enormous boulders. If a ship got through without sinking, he picked it up and made his body glow red hot, causing the ship to burst into flame. Talus was not a living being. He was an automoton, the invention of Hephaestus, the craftsman god who kept his forge on Mount Olympus. Hephaestus made the giant robot as a gift for King Minos, the ruler of Crete. Talus's body was crafted of bronze, and his veins were filled with ichor, a magic fluid that some said was the blood of the gods. The ichor animated the metal giant and made him seem alive. Talus's veins were sealed by a silver nail in his ankle—his only vulnerable spot.

As the *Argo* approached, Talus began his assault. But Medea knew his weakness. She murmured an incantation that caused him to pull the nail from his own ankle. As the ichor drained from his body, Talus collapsed and the *Argo* sailed away. Eventually Jason and Medea arrived in Greece and married. But since murdering her own brother was a horrible crime, the gods made sure that she and her husband were very unhappy. No one knows what became of the fabulous Golden Fleece.

The Minotaur

King Minos of Crete was a cruel tyrant who ruled his island realm from a luxurious palace in the city of Knossos. There he kept a terrible beast called the Minotaur. The monster had the powerful body of a large, muscular man and the head of a bull, with beady red eyes, a fleshy muzzle, and razor-sharp horns. It was vicious, with an enormous appetite for human flesh. Minos kept his appalling pet in an elaborate maze with hundreds of winding corridors leading to the beast's chamber at its center. He named this maze the Labyrinth. No one who entered the complicated maze could find the way out, and Minos kept the Minotaur very well fed by sending victims into the Labyrinth.

Seeking a source of fresh meat for the monster, King Minos sent a messenger to Greece with an ultimatum. He threatened to destroy the city of Athens unless seven youths and maidens were sent each year to be sacrificed to the Minotaur. Theseus, the crown prince of Athens, bravely volunteered to be one of the first seven, for in his heart he had resolved to kill the beast.

When the Greeks arrived in Crete, the king's daughter Ariadne was struck by Theseus's beauty and nobility, so she decided to help the young prince. That night she took him to the portals of the Labyrinth and gave him a sword and a ball of twine. She held one end, and as he made his way through the dark maze, he unwound the twine so that he could follow his trail back to the entrance. For hours Theseus groped this way and that, until he found the lair of the Minotaur. He crept up and slit the monster's throat as it slept. There was no blood, which made the beast seem even more horrible. Theseus followed the twine back to Ariadne, and together they released the other Greeks. Before dawn they all sailed for Athens.

The Gorgon Medusa

On the shores of the western ocean there lived three sisters called Gorgons. Two were hideously ugly, with snouts, bulging eyes, and purple tongues that lolled out between yellow tusks like those of swine. They had bronze claws and great green, scaly wings. The third sister was different. She was beautiful, but poisonous vipers writhed from her scalp instead of hair. Her name was Medusa. She was actually the most terrible of the three, for anyone who glanced upon her face was instantly turned to stone. All around the Gorgons' cave were statues of those who had seen her.

Perseus was a Greek youth, handsome and brave and very proud because his father was Zeus himself. Perseus boasted that he would go and bring back the head of Medusa. Zeus loved his son and sent help from Olympus. Hermes gave Perseus winged sandals so that he might fly and a silver sickle for cutting off the Gorgon's head. Athena, the goddess of wisdom, gave him a shield polished like a mirror. She instructed Perseus to look only upon Medusa's reflection, so that he would not be turned to stone. Then, from the nymphs of the North, he received a magic cap that made him invisible and a pouch for carrying Medusa's head.

Perseus flew on his winged sandals to find the Gorgons. When he saw the statues of those who had glimpsed Medusa, he donned the cap of invisibility and, while looking in the mirrored shield, entered the Gorgons' cave. He came up behind Medusa, sliced off her terrible head with its hissing snakes, and placed it in his pouch. Her horrible sisters shrieked and howled, but the young hero was invisible, so they could do nothing. Perseus presented Athena with Medusa's awful severed head, and forever after the goddess wore the gruesome trophy on her breastplate.

The queen of Tiryns fell in love with Bellerophon, a handsome young man in her husband's court, but he was loyal to his king and would have nothing to do with her. So her love turned to hatred, and she lied to her husband, telling him that the young man was in love with her. In a jealous rage, the king sent Bellerophon to his wife's father, the king of Lycia, with a sealed message that read, "The bearer of these words must be slain."

For years the kingdom of Lycia had been ravaged by a terrible monster. The Chimera was a nightmarish creature. In front it was a vicious lion with savage teeth and claws; in the middle it was an enormous goat with sharp, curving horns; and in the rear it was a huge serpent with poisonous fangs. A fire burned in its belly, and each of its three heads belched flames. Even when the Chimera was resting, noxious smoke drifted from its six nostrils. No weapon could penetrate its thick, leathery hide. The beast had its lair in the mountains above the kingdom, and from time to time it ravaged the valleys where people lived, destroying crops, devouring livestock, and setting houses afire.

The Lycian king decided to send Bellerophon to fight the Chimera. He was certain that the young man would be slaughtered, fulfilling his son-in-law's wish. But the goddess Athena looked down from Olympus and took pity on Bellerophon. She appeared to him in a dream, dressed in gleaming armor, silently holding out a golden bridle studded with precious jewels. When Bellerophon awoke, Athena's bridle was by his side and a magnificent white horse with silvery wings was grazing nearby. The youth slowly walked over to the beautiful creature and slipped the bridle onto its head. Then he mounted his steed and flew off to find the Chimera.

Pegasus, the Winged Horse

Bellerophon's steed was named Pegasus. He had been born when Perseus killed Medusa. Blood gushed from her neck and flowed to the sea, mingling with the waves, and suddenly the winged horse sprang from the surf. Pegasus was wild and spirited, snowy white, with blazing eyes and golden hooves, and his great silvery wings were tipped with golden feathers. After his birth Pegasus soared away to Mount Helicon, the home of the Muses, nine sister goddesses who inspired artists, poets, and musicians. There he struck the earth with his hoof and a clear, sparkling spring bubbled from the rocks. The Muses looked after Pegasus until Athena gave him to Bellerophon.

From his mount on Pegasus high in the sky, Bellerophon found the Chimera by the smoke rising from its cave. He took a piece of lead and attached it to the end of his spear. When the Chimera saw the winged horse, it reared up on its hind legs and vomited flames. Pegasus darted here and there as Bellerophon took aim and shoved his lead-tipped spear deep into the beast's gaping throat. The searing heat melted the lead, choking the monster to death. The king was so impressed and delighted that not only did he allow Bellerophon to live, the young hero was made heir to the throne.

Bellerophon kept Pegasus, and when the king died, he inherited the kingdom of Lycia. But Bellerophon grew conceited and arrogant. He forgot that his good fortune was due to Athena. One day he decided to fly to Mount Olympus itself. Zeus was outraged and sent a horsefly to sting Pegasus. He bucked, and Bellerophon tumbled to earth. He was not killed, but his spirit was broken, and he died a miserable man. Pegasus flew on to Olympus, where he was given the high honor of bearing Zeus's crackling thunderbolts.

Cerberus, the Watchdog of Hades

Deep beneath the earth the dark god Hades ruled over the land of the dead. It was a cold, misty place where dim gray ghosts restlessly drifted about in silence. The gates of this dismal land were guarded by a ferocious watchdog named Cerberus. He was an enormous mastiff with three monstrous heads and a serpent's tail. His jaws were filled with sharp teeth, and he drooled poisonous foam. When the ghost of a newly departed soul arrived, Cerberus let it enter freely. But once inside, the soul was trapped forever, for Cerberus allowed no one to leave. One bite of his vicious, snapping jaws meant an eternity of agony.

Orpheus was the greatest musician in the world. His beautiful music tamed savage beasts. It was said that rocks moved and trees swayed to the sound of his lyre, and his pure voice could even stop rivers from flowing. Orpheus fell deeply in love with a maiden named Eurydice, and she returned his love. But on their wedding day Eurydice was bitten by a viper, and she died. In his grief Orpheus resolved to go down into the underworld to get her back.

As Orpheus approached the gates of Hades, Cerberus pricked his ears and bared his terrible fangs. But Orpheus began to play a mournful dirge, and Cerberus was soon gently wagging his tail like a puppy. Orpheus's song of sorrow was the sweetest music ever heard. Even Hades himself was touched by its beauty, and he allowed Eurydice to return to her life—on one condition: Orpheus was to lead the way, with Eurydice following, and he must not look back. They made their way up and up, but just as Orpheus saw daylight, he could hold back no longer and turned to look. Alas, it was too soon—Eurydice was still in the shadows, and she slipped away. Orpheus never made music again.

The Phoenix

The kingdom of Arabia lay far to the south of Greece. It was a vast desert, scorching hot and bone dry, the domain of tribes who wore billowing robes, lived in tents, and rode camels. The desert was also home to the rarest, most exotic creature in the world. The Phoenix resembled a large eagle, but with magnificent plumage of brilliant purple, scarlet, and yellow. The fabulous bird lived far from human beings in the remotest desert, nesting in the fronds of a palm tree that grew by a pool of crystal-clear water, the sweetest and purest on earth. Each morning at dawn the Phoenix greeted the sun god, Helios, with a melodious call, spreading its splendid wings and bathing in the limpid silvery pool as the sun rose. Helios himself sometimes stopped there to quench his thirst as he began his daily journey through the heavens.

The Phoenix was so rare simply because only one existed at a time. Each Phoenix lived for five hundred years. At the end of its long life it flew to the city of Heliopolis in Egypt—the city of the sun god. There it constructed a mound of cinnamon twigs on the high altar of Helios. Perched atop the aromatic pyre, the great bird spread its feathers and suddenly burst into flames. As it fanned the fire by beating its shimmering wings, the old Phoenix slowly expired in a blaze of glory. Then from the last flickering spark a new Phoenix was born, rising from the ashes fully grown, as resplendent as the old. After the young Phoenix gathered the ashes and buried them, it flew back to its oasis, never to be seen until, once again, its life was nearly over. Then the cycle was repeated. According to legend, the Phoenix will die in flames and be reborn over and over again until the end of time.

EPILOGUE

The golden age of ancient Greece lasted only for a short time—much less than the five-hundred-year life span of a single mythological Phoenix. Eventually Greek civilization was absorbed into the Roman Empire, and Greek mythology was adopted by the people of Rome as their own. The Romans spoke Latin instead of Greek, so they used different names for many of the gods and heroes. Zeus became Jupiter, Hera became Juno, Hermes became Mercury, and Athena became Minerva, but they still looked down upon the world from the summit of Mount Olympus. The Romans took the Phoenix as a symbol of Rome itself, the Eternal City, and as they conquered the world, the Roman legions spread classical civilization and its mythology to every part of the empire. But with the decline and fall of Rome and the rise of Christianity, the ancient gods were abandoned, and the age-old stories no longer told. In time the Greek myths were almost forgotten.

Then, after more than a thousand years, there was a rebirth of classical learning. During a period of history known as the Renaissance the surviving works of the ancient poets, playwrights, painters, and sculptors were rediscovered, and once again the Greek myths were available to inspire artists of all kinds in the creation of new masterpieces. Greek mythology is one of the grandest traditions of Western civilization. We no longer believe in the old gods and heroes, and we know that Gorgons and Minotaurs and winged horses did not exist, but we still find great beauty and profound truths about human nature in the timeless stories that were first told many ages ago. The ancient Greeks had a wonderful notion—the poet flies upon the wings of Pegasus, and in our imaginations so can we.

FOR NICHOLAS

Atheneum Books for Young Readers

An imprint of Simon & Schuster Children's Publishing Division

1230 Avenue of the Americas, New York, New York 10020

Book design by Michael McCartney and Krista Vossen

The text for this book is set in Arrus.

The illustrations for this book are painted in acrylic on canvas.

Mr. Curlee would like to thank Ed Peterson for photographing the paintings.

Manufactured in China

First Edition

2 4 6 8 10 9 7 5 3 1

Library of Congress Cataloging-in-Publication Data

Curlee, Lynn.

Mythological creatures : a classical bestiary / Lynn Curlee.—1st ed.

p. cm.

ISBN-13: 978-1-4169-1453-2

ISBN-10: 1-4169-1453-6

1. Mythology, Classical—Juvenile literature. 2. Bestiaries—Juvenile literature. 3. Animals—Folklore—Juvenile literature.

4. Animals, Mythical—Juvenile literature. I. Title.

BL727.C87 2006

292.2'12—dc22

2006016980